LADYBOY

AN EROTIC ADVENTURE

VICTORIA RUSH

VOLUME 20

JADE'S EROTIC ADVENTURES - BOOK 20

COPYRIGHT

Everybody's an exhibitionist in disguise...

Spying on the neighbors just got a lot more interesting...

Everything's sexier in the dark...

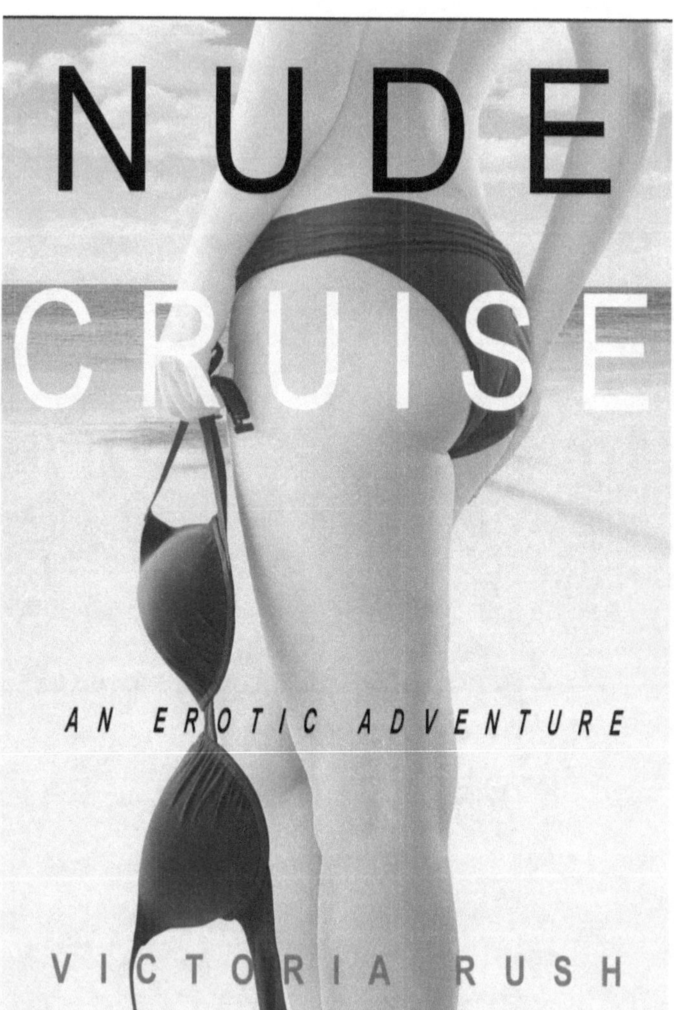

Some people get wet on a cruise for different reasons...

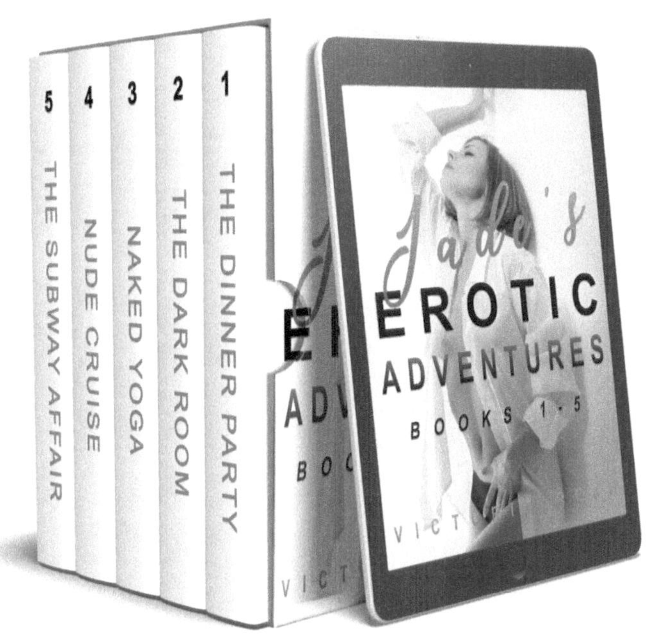

Books 1 -5 in the bestselling series - 60% off

For the uninhibited...

1

I'd been looking forward to this night out for a long time. It had been ages since I'd been out to a show, and the live cabaret act that my best friend Hannah had invited me to promised to be a lot of fun. Starring female impersonators, there'd be plenty of singing, dancing, comedy, and campy good fun.

In the spirit of the theme for the night, Hannah and I had agreed to dress up in cross-gender outfits, and I was eager to see what she'd chosen to wear. I'd found an old padded-shoulder pantsuit in my closet and paired it with a see-through chiffon blouse, skinny red tie and matching high heels. Deciding at the last moment to go topless underneath, the lapels of my blazer and the narrow strip of silk down the front disguised just enough of my bosom to look half-convincingly like a man. To accentuate the appearance, I'd trimmed my hair and slicked it back over my head with some heavy gel. Of course, the six-inch-high Louboutin pumps and my curvy figure in the tight suit left little doubt as to my real identity. But something told me not many people would be looking at my *shoes* this evening.

When my doorbell rang, I finished applying mascara and blush then ran downstairs excitedly to greet Hannah. But as I swung open the door, I gasped and had to hold onto the handle to steady myself. She was wearing a Scottish kilt, replete with high white knee socks, leather sporran, and a glengarry hat. But instead of the usual argyle jacket or waistcoat up top, she wore a thin plaid sash running diagonally over the front of her bare chest. Covering only half of her torso, her right breast poked brazenly out next to the flimsy tartan strip.

"Holy fuck, Hannah!" I said. "I didn't know you were going to go full *Mel Gibson* on me tonight!"

"You *told* me to dress up like a man," she deadpanned.

"Um, well yeah–dressed up in a man's outfit, but not with your *tits* hanging out!"

"Well, technically I've only got *one* tit hanging out," she said, stretching the ribbon to pull it over her other breast. "But at least the sash is pleated, so I can look a little more demure if the mood pleases me.

"Besides," she said, glancing at my see-through blouse. "You're not exactly leaving much to the imagination with that outfit. If it weren't for that skinny tie barely covering your cleavage, you'd be putting most of it out there on display too."

"Not quite as blatantly as you," I huffed, pulling my lapels tighter over my shoulders.

"Come on," she winked. "Tonight's all about having fun, remember? What good is it going to a queer revue if we can't let our hair down?"

"Speaking of," I smiled, tracing her strawberry-colored ringlets down over her bare shoulders. "I like your hairstyle. It goes nicely with the tartan theme."

"Yours too," she said. "Kind of minimalist, but it matches the power suit, and it highlights your cheekbones."

"Thanks," I said, looking at my phone to check the time. "Are you ready to do this? We better leave soon if we're going to get there in time for the start of the show."

"I've been ready all day," she said. "Let's go get our Vogue on."

When we got to the theater, there was already a long line stretched along the side of the building, but we found a spot to park on the side of the street not far away. As we approached the venue, the crowd was pumped up, chatting and joking boisterously in flashy drag costumes. With their heavy makeup, colorful wigs and over-the-top costumes, it was hard to tell the men from the women. Everybody seemed to have gotten into character, mimicking the campy personas of the female impersonators inside.

"Looks like a raucous crowd," I said, pulling up at the end of the line.

"These shows typically involve a lot of audience participation," Hannah nodded. "Kind of like the Rocky Horror Picture Show. That's part of the fun."

I looked up at a neon sign flashing on the brick wall above us.

"'*Lips?*'" I said. "Isn't that a bit of a strange name for a cabaret show?"

"Not for a *queer* cabaret show," Hannah said, smiling at a pretty girl wearing a feather boa next to us in line. "If you think about it, it's actually the perfect name for a female impersonator act. It's mostly about the singing, but it's also a metaphor for a woman's anatomy. These girls take their act pretty seriously."

"Except they're not really *girls*," I chuckled.

"You'll be amazed at how authentic these performers look and sound. You'd never know they were actually men under all their makeup and bodily enhancements."

"Enhancements?"

"Some of these performers take hours to get into drag. Between the makeup, wigs, and all the extra padding, it's quite a production. But the final results are quite astounding. Some of them are actually quite gorgeous."

"You make them sound almost fuckable."

"Well most of them are *men*, after all, under all their entrapments. It's kind of fun imagining taking a pretty girl to bed only to find she's equipped with a real functioning cock."

"Like in the song by Lou Reed, *Take a Walk on the Wild Side*?"

"Yeah, kind of like that."

"You said most of them are men. What about the others?"

"It's hard to say, because everybody's so well camouflaged. They're all *gay* of course, but I suspect there's a fair number of transgender girls who are transitioning one way or the other. That's just another aspect that makes it all the more interesting. You never really know what's going on behind their stage personas. But it's all very inclusive and accepting."

I glanced down the line, surveying the mix of primping and preening theatergoers. Everybody seemed to have taken the theme to heart, dressing in provocative outfits. Whether adorned as a man or a woman, they all looked sexy and hot. As I squinted my eyes trying to decipher each person's gender, my eyes stopped at a platinum blonde dressed in a tight corset with cone-shaped cups and black garter stockings. With her hair pulled back into a tall pony tail and pointy eyebrows, she looked like a dead-ringer for Madonna during her *Blind Ambition* days. She caught me staring at her and shook her chest from side to side, playfully twirling the tassels hanging from the tips of her bra as she smiled at me. I pulled my shoulders back, stretching my suit lapels to reveal the erect nipples showing under my sheer blouse.

"I see what you mean," I said. "I'm already getting excited about meeting some of these girls."

W hen we got inside the theater, the hostess escorted us to a table near the front of the stage and we ordered some cocktails as a loud buzz began to fill the room.

"How'd you score us such primo seats?" I said to Hannah. "I was afraid showing up so late, we'd be stuck in the bleachers."

"Nothing a little extra *lubrication* can't fix," Hannah smiled, rubbing her fingers together, indicating she'd tipped the hostess handsomely. "The closer we can get to the action, the more immersive the experience will be."

"Mmm," I nodded, as the room lights dimmed and a spotlight lit up the stage.

Suddenly a tall redhead wearing a feathery costume with black fishnet stockings and high hells pulled the drapes aside and strutted out onto the stage.

"Good evening, ladies and *wannabees*!" she shouted into the mic. "Are you ready to have some fun?!"

"*Woo hoo!*" the audience wailed, stomping their feet excitedly on the floor.

"My name's Ginger Snaps, and I'll be your MC for the

evening," she said. She placed the side of her hand over her eyebrows and peered out into the crowd. "Do we have any *queens* in attendance tonight?"

Another loud cheer arose from the crowd as many patrons waived their hands proudly over their heads. I peered up and down the MC's figure, inspecting her long slender legs, curvy hips, and full bosom. With her arched eyebrows, pouty lips and bright red wig, she looked just like a sexy, full-blooded woman.

"That's a *man*?" I said, whispering into Hannah's ear.

"Uh-huh," she nodded, smiling up at the MC.

Ginger caught Hannah's gaze and moved closer towards our table.

"I see we have a few other Scarlet O-*Hair*-ahs in the room," she said, flipping her poufy mane dramatically behind her shoulder.

"What's your name, sweetheart?" she said, kneeling down and extending the mic in our direction.

"Hannah," my friend blushed.

"I like your costume," Ginger said. "Goes nicely with your fiery hair. Why don't you stand up and show the audience what you're wearing tonight? Don't be shy, sweetie. We're all queens tonight."

Hannah stood up and turned around, pulling her sash to the side to flash her bare breast then jerked her hips, flipping up the leather pouch between her legs. The crowd hollered its approval and Hannah sat down, as a crimson flush spread over her chest.

"That's pretty hot, honey," Ginger said. "But do the curtains match the carpet under that kilt of yours? Have you got a tinge of the *ginge* in your minge?"

Hannah glanced at me for a moment, contemplating lifting her skirt for everybody to see what lay underneath, but I shook my head in horror, already embarrassed enough by all the attention we were getting from the bright spotlight focused on our table.

"Do you guys want to hear some good redhead jokes?" Ginger said, turning to the crowd.

Everybody hollered in encouragement and Ginger stood back up, raising the mic to her mouth.

"What do you call it when a redhead squirts when she comes?"

"*A Fanta blast.*"

The audience roared in laughter.

"How many redheads does it take to screw in a lightbulb?" Ginger continued.

"*None. They prefer to hide in the dark.*"

Hannah grinned good-naturedly, but I could tell she was beginning to feel the sting from the pointed jokes.

"What's the difference between a ginger and a brick?" Ginger said.

"*At least the brick gets laid.*"

Hannah placed her hands on her hips and pouted, pretending to be hurt.

"But that's not true, is it Hannah?" Ginger said. "We gingers know better. We get plenty of action. You've heard of *yellow fever* for people who like to have sex with Asians? Except in our case, the obsession with carrot tops is called *gingivitis.*"

As the crowd chuckled and howled, Ginger finally turned away from our table and motioned toward the red velvet curtain at the back of the stage.

"Enough redhead jokes," she said. "Who's ready for some *diva delights!?*"

"Woo hoo!" the audience hollered.

"Well then, let's hear a big round of applause for the hottest girls this side of the Mississippi!"

She waved her hand toward the curtain, and it suddenly parted as five flamboyant girls strutted forward in unison singing *It's Raining Men.*

Hi, hi, we're your weather girls and we've got news for you, they warbled.

As they swiveled their bodies in harmony to the women's empowerment anthem, I ran my eyes over their sexy figures. Every one of them had long slim legs, curvy hips with narrow waists, and full, realistic bosoms. As they belted out the song in full soprano voices, I watched their lips trying to detect if they were lip-syncing to the music. But I didn't notice any gaps or disconnects between what their mouths were saying and what the music was projecting.

I turned to look at Hannah, dumbfounded. Besides having pitch-perfect, exquisite feminine voices, every one of them was drop-dead gorgeous.

"You've *got* to be kidding me," I shouted over the music. "You can't be serious that these are *men* dressed up as women?!"

"I told you they took their act serious," Hannah nodded. "They go to extraordinary lengths to play their part convincingly."

"But," I protested. "Their legs, their asses, their *breasts.* They look like real women!"

"It's part diet, part genetics, and the rest is just good makeup."

"But those hips! And their tits! How can they make them look so real?"

"It's amazing what a little bit of strategically placed padding and waist-cinching will do. Do you like it?"

"I guess so," I said. "I mean, there's no denying that they're all hot. It's just weird knowing they're actually men underneath all that makeup."

We've got news for you, you better listen up, the girls continued singing.

"Don't think about any of that," Hannah said. "Just sit back and lose yourself in the fantasy. Enjoy the ride!"

I nodded at Hannah, then turned back to watch the performers.

Get ready all you lonely girls, they sang.

And leave your umbrellas at home...

As they twisted their bodies and shook their hips to the beat, I watched the muscles in their arms and legs, looking for the telltale signs of any masculine features. But their limbs were smooth and slim, and their calves as long and skinny as any woman's. Even their tits and asses giggled like a real woman's. As each girl took a turn singing a solo part, I studied her facial expression and skin tone, looking for any evidence of a five o'clock shadow.

'Cause tonight, for the first time in history, a sexy brunette wailed,

it's gonna start raining men.

As they all joined together in formation to sing the song's chorus, moving to within a few feet of our table, I felt goosebumps from the excitement of witnessing such an electrifying performance.

It's raining men, hallelujah, it's raining men, they trilled.

I'm gonna go out to run and let myself get wet, absolutely soaking wet.

As I began to get caught up in the act, a strange feeling came over me. Even though I identified as a lesbian, I was beginning to get wet myself watching these female impersonators shaking their sexy bodies and singing such an empowering song. By the time the song was over and the MC came back out to work the crowd with some more light-hearted jokes, I was already shifting uncomfortably in my seat, feeling the wetness in my tight-fitting pants spreading down my thighs.

"Pretty sexy, huh?" Hannah said, noticing my disequilibrium. "Bet you never thought you'd get this excited watching a bunch of guys performing on stage."

"I still can barely believe it," I said. "They just don't have any of the normal manly features. No sinewy muscles, broad shoulders, or square jawlines..."

"I suspect a lot of them are drawn to this line of work because they're already blessed with naturally effeminate features. If you look closely, you can see their Adam's Apples when they turn a certain way. But who cares, anyway? All the power to them if they can entertain a whole room full of admirers to this degree."

"They're *entertaining*, alright," I said, adjusting my tight pants bunching up around my moist crotch.

"Don't tell me you're actually getting *turned on* watching these guys?" Hannah said, raising an eyebrow. "I thought you just liked women?"

"I do, for the most part. I guess my mind is just playing tricks with my body. When they're doing their schtick, I can't help imagining them as sexy women."

"I suppose they've accomplished their goal then," Hannah nodded. "For all intents and purposes, when they're on stage, they *are* women."

The MC suddenly raised the volume of her voice, interrupting us.

"What do you guys think?" she said. "*Are you ready for some more T-girl action!?*"

As the crowd roared, she stepped toward the side of the stage, swinging her arm back toward the red curtain.

"Let's spice it up then!"

The curtain parted again, and the five performers sashayed slowly onto the stage, while the music from the Spice Girls' hit song *2 Become 1* filled the room. As the opening verse started, one of the girls separated from the rest, slinking toward the front of the podium. Everyone had changed their costumes to look like one of the original Spice Girls, and this time it was 'Sporty Spice's' turn to introduce the song.

Candlelight and soul forever, she purred.

A dream of you and me together,

Say you believe it, say you believe it...

I marveled at how beautiful and authentic her voice was, and before long I found myself swooning at the intoxicating lyric.

Next, it was the Scary Spice character's turn, looking for all the world like a young Mel B in her caramel-colored afro wig.

Free your mind of doubt and danger, she crooned.

Be for real, don't be a stranger,

We can achieve it, we can achieve it...

I'd always thought Scary Spice was the sexiest Spice Girl, and as she warbled the suggestive lyrics, I crossed my legs together, squeezing my throbbing clit, remembering how I'd fawned over her as an adoring adolescent. By the time her set had finished, I was feeling so hot I had to take my blazer off and hang it over the back of my chair to let my body breathe. With the spotlight focused on the girls on the stage, I felt confident in the shadows that no one would notice my rapidly hardening nipples under my flimsy see-through blouse.

But it was the *next* performer that really got my juices going. As the spotlight swung to the other side of the stage, the performer resembling Baby Spice began singing the next verse. With her parted pony tails and tight lamé dress, I practically melted when she began walking toward our table and locked eyes on me.

Come a little bit closer baby, get it on, get it on, she teased.

'Cause tonight is the night when two become one...

As I stared at her with wide fawning eyes, she gazed at my chest, noticing my nipples protruding like doorbell buttons under the glow of the spotlight cascading toward our table. By the time she'd finished singing her part, I'd already begun to fantasize about joining together with her every way I could. But as much as I tried, I couldn't see any sign of an Adam's Apple in her throat while she flexed her muscles belting out the song. Even her *hands* looked feminine and petite as she caressed the microphone erotically, tormenting me with her dark brown eyes. When the five girls came back together and began to sing the chorus, I'd already transported myself back twenty years when I used to fantasize as a teenager about making love to each of the Spice Girls one at a time.

I need some love like I never needed love before, they sang.

Wanna make love to ya baby,

Wanna make love to ya baby,

Set your spirit free, it's the only way to be.

Even though each of the T-girls had her own individual vibe going on, there was only one I was fixated on now. As I watched Baby Spice mouth the words sexily to me, I felt the puddle between my legs expand further and further down my pant leg, and it took everything in my power not to mouth the words back to her.

I want to make love to you too, baby, I dreamed.

2

———

For many days after the cabaret show, I dreamed about the sexy T-girls prancing around the stage, crooning their songs as they took turns shimmying up to my table and peering into my eyes. I imagined going to bed with each one, but in every case I ended up disappointed when they disrobed and revealed their fake padding and flapping dicks. It wasn't so much that I was turned off by them being men under their suggestive costumes–after all, I'd enjoyed my fair share of hard cocks in my life. It was that the fantasy bubble I'd created in my mind's eye had been so rudely popped.

But my thoughts kept returning to the pretty blonde one who seemed so much more feminine than the rest. Even though Hannah had warned me that she was probably just another gay guy dressed up in a convincing outfit, I wanted to *believe* that she was something more. Maybe it was the sweet Spice Girls character she played in one of her sets that had got me going, but there was something about her that I found different, and highly alluring.

I was already planning to go back to the venue to take in

their next show and wait by the exit door after the performance to see if I could catch sight of her out of costume. I wasn't sure how or whether I could approach her, I just needed to know one way or the other what her deal was. I knew that I was probably deluding myself into thinking we'd made any kind of meaningful connection during her performance, knowing that she, like most of the rest of the performers, was just play-acting for the benefit of their fans' prurient fantasies. But my steadily throbbing pussy whenever I thought of her told me I couldn't let it go.

Trying to take my mind off my never-ending obsession, I decided to go grocery shopping at my local supermarket to find a temporary distraction. When I walked into the store and saw all the bright produce displayed on the stands and smelled the aroma of freshly baked bread, I smiled knowing this was just the remedy I needed. Collecting the ingredients for a home-cooked meal would soon refocus my attention on my rumbling stomach instead of my other aching body part.

As I began assembling the ingredients for a cucumber salad, I couldn't help imagining each item as a symbol for the female impersonators I'd seen a few days before. I picked up a large red onion and squeezed it to make sure it was properly firm, wondering if their silicone implants felt equally hard. Then I ambled over to the refrigerated display case and lifted a tuft of fresh dill to my nose. It smelled grassy with a hint of licorice, and I closed my eyes wondering if that's the way my Baby Spice T-girl might smell if I got her naked.

Naked, nothing but a smile upon her face, I hummed the melody to their hit song Naked.

I grabbed some garlic powder, sour cream and white vinegar to make the dressing, then angled back to the produce section to pick up some radishes and cucumbers. As I approached the cucumber stand, I smiled inspecting the long green tubers which always reminded me of a certain well-hung porn star. I occasionally liked to use English cucumbers as a substitute for rubbery vibrators, reveling in the natural texture and flexibility of the phallic-shaped objects. I picked up one of the larger ones and bent it sensuously in my hands, sensing another customer hovering behind me, waiting for me to finish fondling the merchandise.

"Are you more interested in *length* or *girth*?" she said with a sultry voice.

I swung around to see a pretty blonde woman about my height, smiling at me as I held the long vegetable upright in my hand.

"Oh, ah, *yeah*," I stammered. "It *does* have a certain suggestive shape, doesn't it?"

"I prefer zucchini squash, myself," she said, running her fingers delicately over my cucumber's shaft. "It's a little shorter and stubbier, but it has that lovely bulbous tip that makes it feel a little more authentic."

I blushed, suddenly feeling embarrassed by her cheeky manner.

"Oh, I'm just planning to use this to make a *cucumber salad*," I lied.

"Whatever you say, sweetie," she smiled. "It works well for *that* too."

I darted my eyes back and forth across her face, recognizing something familiar.

"Do I know you from somewhere?" I said. "It feels like I've seen you before."

"I don't think we've met," she said, holding out her hand. "My name's Shae. But I get around quite a bit, so there's a good chance we've crossed paths one place or another."

"Jade," I said, I squinting my eyes trying to place the recollection.

Then my eyes suddenly flew open. Her pointy nails gave it away. *It was Baby Spice from the cabaret show*! And she looked even prettier and sexier in street clothes. Wearing a tight wool sweater and skinny jeans, I ran my eyes shamelessly over her curvy figure.

"Oh my God!" I gushed. "You're one of those girls from the *Lips Cabaret Show*, aren't you? I barely recognized you out of costume. I absolutely *loved* your act! If you don't mind my saying, I thought you were one of the sexiest performers."

"Thank you," she said, lowering her voice. "I try to keep a low profile when I leave the stage. There's a lot of fanatics out there who are obsessed with T-girls. You never know when you might run into someone who's got a more insidious intention in mind..."

"Sorry," I apologized. "I didn't mean to invade your privacy. You must get accosted everywhere you go..."

"It's okay, honey. You're one of the few people who've recognized me offstage. And besides," she said, scanning my pointy nipples pressing against my cotton T-shirt. "You don't strike me as one of the dangerous types." She glanced around her, noticing other supermarket customers eyeing us suspiciously. "Why don't we continue this conversation in a quieter place? There's a Starbucks just a few blocks down the street."

S hae and I drove our separate cars to the coffee shop, then we went inside and ordered a pair of lattes, finding a quiet table in the corner to chat.

"I hope you don't mind my asking," I said, pulling up a chair. "You don't seem like the other performers. I mean, you look like a–"

"*Woman*?" she chuckled. "Most of us girls put on a pretty convincing act. It's all part of the game. It takes quite a few hours behind the scenes to get into character."

"It doesn't look like you need much *help*," I said, still intrigued by her evasive answer. "You're already gorgeous and plenty curvy..."

"I guess I've been blessed with some natural genetics," she said. "Some of my gay friends have to work a little harder to create the look. May I ask what brought you to our show? Were you just looking for a little fun, or are you another one of those drag queen groupies?"

"I guess I was looking for a little change of pace. I've been flitting from one flighty relationship to another, and I needed a little distraction..."

"Are you attracted to *T-girls*?" Shae asked. "How do you identify, sexually?

"I've tried it both ways," I said. "But I seem to have settled into a comfortable groove with other women. Though I *have* had the occasional fling with a transitional girl."

"*Oh*?" Shae said, raising an eyebrow. "Which way? I mean, was she transitioning from a boy to a girl or a girl to a boy?"

"Boy to girl, I think. She looked for all intents like a woman, but still had all the functioning boy parts."

"Did you *like* having it both ways?" she smiled.

"It was definitely interesting," I nodded, happy to see her

becoming more interested in my sex life. "Ever since then, I've been kind of intrigued with the whole *ladyboy* thing, if I can use that term. I even dressed up at a masquerade ball once wearing a strap-on dildo, and I've fantasized more than once about being one for real."

"It sounds like you're a little obsessed with ladyboys," Shae said, running her eyes over my chest. "I think I remember you now. You were the hot chick sitting near the front of the stage with the slicked-back hair and the chiffon blouse. I'd recognize those tips anywhere."

"Yeah, sorry," I said. "It was getting a little hot in there and you were kind of getting me worked up–"

"Maybe that's why you came to the show," she grinned. "To live out your fantasies of getting it on with a real T-girl?"

"I dunno," I said. "There's something strangely arousing about being with a transsexual person. I get to imagine them as a woman while still experiencing the act of penetration..."

"Mmm," Shae nodded, adjusting her position in her chair, obviously getting as excited as I was by our conversation. "You're not alone. There's a whole subculture of futa-loving fanatics out there. Both men and women."

"Does that make me a freak or something?" I said. "It doesn't quite seem normal..."

"No less than the people plying their wares on the other side of the coin. Everything's pretty gender-fluid these days. Nobody can seem to make up their minds what they want to be, or who they want to be with."

"You almost make it sound like a *bad* thing," I said, still searching for clues as to her real sex. "How did you get into this line of work anyhow?"

"I kind of fell into it. I have a lot of gay and bisexual friends and when I went to my first T-girl revue, they thought I'd be a natural at it. It's kind of fun to vamp it up and put on a different persona for a bunch of adoring fans. I find it very invigorating to receive that kind of affirmation from the crowd."

"How do you identify *yourself*, if you don't mind my asking?" I said, growing more confident with her increasing transparency. "I mean, do you consider yourself gay, bi, or trans?"

"I prefer not to pigeonhole myself into any particular corner," she said, placing her elbows on the table and leaning forward to gaze into my eyes. "I consider myself *pansexual*-I enjoy having sex with anyone who turns my crank."

"I feel exactly the same way," I smiled, sensing an opportunity to move our conversation to the next level. "Are you feeling hungry? Maybe we can get out of this place and find a bite to eat."

"I'm absolutely famished," she said. "I could really go for a cucumber salad about now."

"Oh?" I said, raising an eyebrow playfully. "Would you like to come back to my place? It would be a shame to waste all those tasty vegetables on just myself."

"I thought you'd never ask," Shae said. "But something tells me you won't need that cucumber after all. I think we might find some *other* ways to satisfy our appetite..."

The moment we got to my place and I set the grocery bags down in my kitchen, Shae and I fell into each other's arms as we groped each other and pressed our bodies together against the island. I could feel her tits mashing against mine and all I wanted to do was get her naked as quickly as possible to ravish her body. Besides, I was dying to see what she'd been hiding so carefully from me ever since we met. I still wasn't sure if she was a natural woman, a pretty boy pretending to be a woman, or someone transitioning from one gender to another.

"Let's go upstairs where we can get more comfortable," I said. "I'm dying to touch you *everywhere*."

"Same here," Shae panted. "I want to have you every way I can."

I held her face, plunging my tongue into her mouth, then grabbed her hand, pulling her down the hall and up the stairs into my master bedroom. We both dropped down onto the bed and I ended up lying next to her with her back leaning against my front side. Feeling all the more excited still not knowing what I'd find, I began taking off her clothes.

I reached around and pulled off her sweater then unclasped her bra, squeezing her breasts tightly in my hands. They felt full and natural, and I ran my fingers around the base of her mounds, trying to feel for the telltale ridge of a silicone implant. But they felt as soft and natural as any woman's. Then I lifted my fingers and rolled them gently over her areolas as she sighed and arched her back in pleasure.

No sign of scars either, I thought. *Whoever did her boobs must have been a very skilled surgeon.*

As I traced my fingers down her quivering abdomen, her skin felt as smooth and soft as a baby's. I didn't detect any sign of hard abdominal muscles or any stubble from recently trimmed hair. I could even feel the thin indentation of her linea alba running down the middle of her stomach, something I'd always found attractive in fit women. As I traced the line toward her crotch with my middle finger, she grabbed my hand and stopped me just above the top of her jean's waistline.

Instead, she slowly unclasped the button and pulled her jeans down over her hips, then shimmied out of her panties and threw them near the base of the bed. Shae was now completely naked facing away from me, and I could feel her hot body radiating next to me. I was dying to reach around and touch her loins to see what surprises lay in wait for me, but I decided to go slow and torment her just as much as she was me.

She pulled her right knee forward, separating her legs a few inches, and I caressed the inside of her thigh from the base of her knee all the way up to her curvy, tight buttocks. I felt a slippery film of fluid as I got close to her crease, and I rubbed my fingers and together, trying to divine its source. It didn't feel thick and mucousy like a man's precum, and I pressed my hips harder against her ass, rejoicing in the knowledge that I was holding a real woman in my arms.

She turned her head around and we kissed softly while I caressed the curvature of her ass, inching my hand toward her steaming cleft. When I felt her slippery slit, I pressed two fingers deep inside her hole, and she moaned into my mouth as our tongues swirled together in delight. As I began to fuck her with my fingers, she rocked her hips along with me, and I felt her juices begin to trickle down over my knuckles. Eager to please her even more, I removed my fingers and traced them forward along her valley, seeking to caress the sensitive nub at the top of the fold.

But when I reached the base of her mound, instead of finding a little clit, I felt a huge, throbbing phallus pointing upward toward her stomach. Hardly believing what I was feeling, I placed my fingers around the shaft and squeezed it tightly to see if it was real. Unlike any strap-on dildo or faux penis I'd ever felt before, this one felt warm and spongy in my hand. And unlike the plastic or silicone fake dicks, this one *pulsed* in my hand as I felt the rush of blood coursing through its shaft.

I suddenly felt a charge of electricity running through my body, realizing I was lying next to a true hermaphrodite for the first time in my life. My pussy gushed in excitement as I traced my fingers further up her shaft, feeling the flare of the coronal ridge encircling the crown at the tip of her cock. Her head was coated in a viscous layer of precum, and she groaned as I swirled my fingers over the sensitive tissue.

"Oh my God, Shae," I whispered. "I had no idea–"

"You said you had a *thing* for ladyboys," she smiled, turning around to face me directly. "Well now you've got your wish. The real question is, have you got the skills to take full advantage of my special equipment?"

"*Fuck* yes," I growled, ripping off my clothes, pressing my tingling body up against hers.

3

"What do you feel like first?" Shae smiled after I'd removed all my clothes. "There's a lot to choose from."

"Mmm," I purred. "Indeed there is. Do you mind if I play with your big thumper first? I've never experienced a real cock attached to a girl before. Just plastic dildos and other artificial toys–"

"Like long *cucumbers*?"

"Ha, yeah–sometimes. But it's not quite the same," I purred, stroking the underside of her shaft with my fingers. "This one you can actually *feel*..."

"Yes, I can," she sighed. "Have at it. That's all anybody seems to want, anyways."

I lifted my hand from Shae's crotch and looked into her eyes, realizing I was treating her like a piece of meat.

"I'm sorry," I said, pulling away. "I imagine this can be awkward for you sometimes. With your fans already expecting to find boy parts under your clothes, they must be even *more* obsessed with your body when they discover you're more than you seem."

"You mean a full-fledged *tranny*?" Shae said. "*Dick girl*? Anatomical *freak*?"

"No," I said, caressing her face softly with my fingers. "I'd never call you any of those things. To me, you're just a girl with a bit of a...*twist*. A very sexy, *surprising* twist."

"Mmm," Shae said, leaning in to kiss me back. "I like the sound of that. I didn't mean to sound so defensive. It's just that I kind of–*like* you. I was hoping we'd have something a little more meaningful than a quick fling."

"I feel the same way," I said. "We can slow down if you want and take some time to get to know one another before we escalate things any further. I've got some food downstairs if you're hungry–"

"No," she said, pressing her hips against me, coating my belly with her dripping cock. "I only want *you* right now. I want to feel your lips all over my body..."

"With pleasure," I purred, kissing my way down her neck. As my face nestled between her cleavage, she arched her back and moaned.

"Suck my tits, Jade," she mewed. "Take my girls into your mouth and tease them like you do your other lovers. Make me feel like a real woman."

"You *are* a real woman to me Shae," I said, peering up at her. "I love your body–*every* part of your body."

I traced my hands down over her shoulders and encircled her full breasts, squeezing them gently. Then I lifted my head and sucked on each of her nipples, making a playful popping sound.

"Yes," Shae moaned. "That feels so good. You're not like most of my other lovers. They just want to *fuck* me or have me fuck them. I like the way you make love to my whole body."

"Mmm," I hummed as I swirled my tongue over her fat

teats. I could feel them lengthening in my mouth and I sucked on them like lollypops as she writhed in delight on the bed.

"I need you Jade," she groaned. "My *cock* needs you. Make love to the rest of my body the way you're worshipping my tits."

I didn't need any further encouragement, and as I slid my body down the front of her slippery abdomen, I pointed her member between my breasts and pressed them together, feeling her heat throbbing between my flesh. The precum dribbling down the underside of her shaft provided ample lubrication, and I proceeded to caress her cock with my melons as she rocked her hips in pleasure.

"Oh God, Jade," she moaned, lifting her head to watch her purple tip poking in and out of my cleft. "I love fucking your tits. You look incredibly hot."

"So do you," I smiled, watching her big pole sliding between my cleavage.

Part of me wanted to continue fucking her with my tits, intrigued to see if or how much she could cum when she reached orgasm. But by now I was burning up with desire also, and I had to feel her in my mouth. I wanted to make love to her most sensitive part and feel her jetting inside me when she came. I lowered my body a few more inches, kneeling between her legs, and looked up at her with a devilish grin. Her pole was bouncing in excitement between her legs, and I grasped it with two hands, beginning to jerk her off slowly.

As she threw her head back in ecstasy, I watched her body writhing on the bed. There was something incredibly erotic about watching a beautiful woman squirming in pleasure while I felt her burning sex in my hands. It was strange to see her breasts jiggling on her chest as I stroked her cock with both hands, her nipples peering up at me like two beacons in the dark shadows of my bedroom.

"Jade," she panted. "You're going to make me come soon. I've never had someone give me such a delicate hand job before. Look into my eyes when I come. I want to see your pretty face."

"Yes, Shae," I hissed, feeling my own juices beginning to run down the inside of my thighs. "Come for me, baby. I want to watch you cum in my hands."

Shae began rocking her hips more urgently then she slammed her hands down onto the bed, clenching the covers between her fingers as she curled her body up toward me, staring into my eyes. Suddenly her cock erupted, spewing ropes of cum all over my tits and face, as I gushed simultaneously all over the sheets. The intense eroticism of watching her beautiful body come alive as I held her tightly in my hands had turned me on so much that I'd come along with her even without any direct stimulation.

As I watched Shae's chest heaving in excitement as she recovered from her powerful climax, we clasped hands, and she pulled me down gently on top of her.

"That was incredible," she panted. "I've never had someone touch me like that before."

I lay down beside her, pushing some loose strands of hair back over her face.

"You've never had someone give you a hand job before?" I asked.

"Not like *that*," she said. "Usually they just want to see me cream, like I'm some kind of robot. But this time it felt like you were making love to me with your eyes. Knowing you were watching me that way made me cum a thousand times harder."

"I could tell," I said, wiping some of her cum off the

side of my face with the back of my hand. "I enjoyed watching you respond to my touch just as much as you did."

Shae slid her knee forward, feeling the big wet spot I'd made on the sheets.

"So it would appear," she said, wiping my face to remove the last traces of cum from my skin. "I've never seen a woman squirt so much before."

"You're not the *only* one with special powers," I smiled.

Shae grabbed my head and thrust her tongue deep into my mouth, pressing her dripping cock up against my stomach.

"I want to return the favor now," she said. "It's *my* turn to watch you while I give you some pleasure."

"I won't say no to that," I purred, rubbing my slippery tits against hers. "What did you have in mind exactly? Like you said, the combinations and permutations are practically limitless."

"As much as I'd like to focus entirely on you, I desperately need to make love to you. I want to be *inside you* this time when we come together."

"Mmm," I smiled, grabbing her ass and pulling her tighter toward me. I felt her burning cock resting against my abdomen, and I swiveled my hips to see if she was still hard. "Are you ready to go at it again this quickly?"

"I've been ready from the moment I met you," she said. "As long as you're lying naked next to me, I don't think there's any risk of my cock flagging."

I reached between our two bodies and squeezed her throbbing member in my hand.

"Should we be taking any precautions?" I said, pinching my eyebrows.

"You mean regarding pregnancy?" she said. "We don't

have to worry about any of that. As you can see, I don't have any balls, so I can't produce sperm."

"But you produced plenty of fluid–"

"That comes from something else. Just like a man, I've got a prostate and seminal vesicles. Ninety percent of a man's ejaculate is produced by those glands–it's just that in my case it's *all* of the cream."

I pulled back momentarily, intrigued to learn more about her unique features.

"What about the rest of the package, if you don't mind my asking?" I said. "You seem to have all the other lady parts. Do you have a uterus and ovaries, like a regular woman?"

"The chromosomes got a little mixed up in my case," Shae said, shaking her head. "I got a little bit of this and a little bit of that when they were handing out the DNA. Every intersex person is born differently. Some have mostly boy parts, some have mostly female parts, and some have a few parts of each."

"Well, I think God endowed you with the *best* combination of parts," I said, tracing a line down the side of her jaw with my finger. "I can't imagine a more perfect specimen than you. You look more beautiful than any woman I've met, and you *still* get to have it both ways."

Shae chuckled softly, then her expression turned more solemn.

"For the longest time, I felt like a freak. When you're a kid, you want to be like all the other kids. But I've learned to make peace with my situation and I hardly think twice about it anymore. I'm just Shae–unique and special in my own way."

"I couldn't have said it better myself," I said, beginning to feel closer to her as she grew increasingly candid. "But I know there's a lot of gender-confused people out there, even without your ambiguous anatomy. Did you ever consider–"

"Surgery?" Shae said. "Not for a moment. I kind of *enjoy* having two sets of organs to play with. You have no idea how much experimenting I did growing up."

"I can imagine," I smiled, thinking about all the different ways I'd found to self-pleasure myself. "But what about your parents? Didn't they want you to fit within society's expected stereotypes? Wasn't there a lot of pressure to choose one clear sex or another?"

"Thankfully, I had pretty progressive parents," Shae nodded. "They loved me for who I am and never pressured me one way or the other. I can't imagine being any different than the way I turned out."

"Neither can I," I said. "I love you just the way you are."

"*Love*?" Shae said teasingly. "Isn't it a bit early to be using those kinds of words? I mean, I just *met* you..."

"I know," I said. "But it feels like I've known you my whole life. There's something deeply spiritual about you. You're unlike any other woman I've met before–"

"That's because you've never met another woman with a real cock before."

"That's not what I mean," I said. "I just feel a special connection with you. I knew you were different the moment I laid eyes on you. I've fantasized about being with you ever since the cabaret show–"

"Being with me, or *being* with me?" Shae said, furrowing her brows. "I don't want you to love me the way all those other ladyboy fanatics do."

I shook my head as I wrapped my arms around her back and pulled her closer.

"I know it's weird to say so soon after we've met, but I

want to be with you forever. As friends, partners, lovers. I'm stuck on you like no one I've met in a long time."

"I feel it too," Shae said, gazing into my eyes. "Let me make love to you properly now. I'm thinking of *another* way for you to be stuck on me."

"Mmm, I like the sound of that," I said, rolling on top of her. "Stick me with that big cock of yours. I want to feel you creaming inside me this time."

Shae tried to turn me over so she could be in the superior position, but I pinned her arms on the bed and smiled mischievously at her.

"Let me be on top. I want to watch you when we join our bodies. *All* of you."

"Same here," Shae smiled. "This time I want to watch you to gush all over my cock when you come."

"Damn straight, girl," I said, rubbing her throbbing pole against my wet labia. "This time I'm going to surround your cock with a *different* part of my anatomy."

"*Yesss*," Shae purred. "Fuck me, Jade. Fuck me with your wet pussy."

I lifted my hips over her quivering dick, then I pointed it toward my hole and slowly lowered myself over her shaft. As she penetrated deep inside me, we both groaned in pleasure. It felt strange having a woman's cock inside me, not just because of the absence of testicles slapping against my ass. The combination of her pretty face, sexy tits, and throbbing hard-on was something I'd never experienced before. As I began to pump my body up and down over her throbbing organ, I gasped when I felt her reach the end of my tunnel.

"*Fuck*, Shae," I groaned. "I've never felt so filled up like this before. Fuck me with that big tool of yours."

Shae grabbed my hips on either side and pulled me

harder toward her as she began thrusting deeper inside me. I tilted forward and grabbed her tits, squeezing them tightly. It was nice to have something substantial to hold on to while I bounced on her joystick, and we both smiled at how perfectly we'd melded together.

"I love looking at your pretty face while I fuck you," I purred, gazing into her eyes as my juices dribbled down over her slit and between her ass.

"I want to look into your eyes when you come this time," Shae said. "I haven't felt this close to anyone in a long time. Make love to me, baby."

I lifted my arms and held my hands out to her, and she grasped my hands again, interlocking her fingers tightly with mine. As we rocked our hips together, gazing lovingly into one another's eyes, our grip grew progressively tighter the closer we edged toward orgasm.

"Fuck, Jade," Shae hissed. "You feel so good. Squeeze my cock with your tight pussy. I want to watch your tits shaking over top of me when you come with me."

"Yes, baby," I panted. "I'm almost there. Pound me with your big dick. Let me feel you spurting inside me."

"Oh God, Jade," Shae grunted. "It's coming. Look at me while I come inside you. Oh *fuckkk...*"

Shae squeezed my fingers so tightly they began to turn blue and her whole body began shaking as she fell over the precipice. With her tits shaking in orgasmic tremors, I arched my back, pointing the tip of her cock against the G-spot on the front side of my pussy. As I watched her mouth gape open in the throes of a powerful climax, I clenched down hard on her pulsating prick and sprayed all over her quivering pussy. Feeling me come on her slit, she angled her hips toward me, jetting her cum hard against my cervix. Feeling her touching my furthest reaches heightened my pleasure all the more, and I shuddered in joy as we gripped each other's hands and peered at one another with watery eyes.

As I collapsed on top of her feeling her warm body pressed against mine, I closed my eyes and rested my head on her chest. For the first time in ages, I felt like I'd found my soulmate.

4

For many long moments, Shae and I lay next to one another, softly caressing each other's skin. I could feel her heart pounding next to my head on her chest, and I wasn't sure if it was because she was still coming down from her high, or if it signaled her joy at being next to me. Either way, I smiled, knowing we'd made a powerful connection and that this was just the start of something wonderful. After a few minutes, I felt her heartbeat returning to normal, and I peered up at her.

"How are you feeling?" I said.

She peered into my eyes and smiled.

"Happy. Content. Euphoric."

"It's probably just the endorphins still floating around your system," I said.

"No," she said, shaking her head. "It's much more than that. With all my other partners, it was mostly about the sex. Like they were using me as a novel plaything. But with you, I can feel something special. I haven't felt this close to anyone in a long time."

"Did you know there's a special hormone that's released

when we have an orgasm with someone? It's called oxytocin, sometimes referred to as the love hormone. It creates feelings of belongingness between partners and promotes a sense of togetherness. Psychologists believe it's an evolutionary adaptation in humans to encourage couples to stay together long enough to raise their children. I've often thought it plays an important role in same-sex relationships too."

"Oxycontin?"

"No," I chuckled. "That's a whole other type of drug. That one produces an intense artificial high, much like heroin. This one's all natural and lasts a much longer time."

"Are you saying these feelings we're developing for one another aren't *real*? That it's just due to the hormones produced when we have sex?"

I could feel Shae's heart racing again under my ear, and I reached up to squeeze her hand reassuringly.

"No, I just think it's interesting how it's all interconnected. How sex and love are mutually interdependent. But true lasting love is something that develops over time. You have to work at it. It's a give-and-take process, where each partner supports one another as they learn each other's wants and desires and learn how to make each other happy in more substantial ways."

"Well if love depends on sex, and sex depends on love," Shae mused, "and the strength of our bond depends on getting to know each other's desires better, then we better get *busy*. Tell me what you like–in *bed*, I mean. What turns you on?"

"Until I met you, I thought I knew. But you're kind of a game-changer. Suddenly, I have so many more...*options*."

"Because I have a cock?"

"Kind of. With other girls, it was all about tribbing and

licking and that sort of thing. You know, mostly focusing on the external organs. But with you, I can feel you *inside* me. I've got a whole new exciting toy to play with. Now I can throw away all my vibrators and dildos–"

"Not so fast," Shae smiled. "I enjoy playing with those things as much as you do. Sometimes it's just as much fun to watch your partner pleasure herself. Besides, I can think of a number of ways we can incorporate those into our sex life to keep it fresh and exciting. Starting with that big vegetable of yours..."

Shae's mention of the cucumber got me thinking about all the new ways I could use it with her. After all, she also had a fully functioning *vagina*, and there was nothing I loved more than using a double-sided dildo with my partner while we ground our pussies together. Only this time, I could watch and play with her pecker too while we fucked each other.

"Mmm," I said. "I like the sound of that. Shall I run downstairs and bring it up for us to play with? I want to fuck you so bad right now."

"In a little while, maybe," Shae said. "First, I want to taste you and make love to you with my mouth. I'm dying to suck your pussy."

My cunny suddenly twitched at the thought of her going down on me.

"I've been dying to take you into my mouth too," I said. "Maybe we can do it at the *same time*. Do you feel like a little sixty-nine action?"

Suddenly Shae's heart began thumping rapidly against the side of my face again.

"Yes," she nodded. "We'll be able to rub our bodies together and hold each other close that way. *Fuck*, yes. I want to bury my face between your legs."

I lifted myself off her body and turned around, lying beside her on the bed with our faces positioned in front of each other's crotch. Her flagpole was already ramrod straight and bobbing inches away from my mouth. I grabbed it gently with my fingers and rolled my tongue around her crown in slow circles.

"Oh God," Shae groaned. "Lick my cock, Jade. Make love to me with your mouth. I'm gonna suck your pussy and taste your honey. I want to feel you gush all over my face when you come this time."

I spread my legs and felt Shae's face press against my dripping hole as she began lapping her way up toward my clit.

"Yes, baby," I panted. "Lick my pussy. Taste my love for you while I suck you off. I love your beautiful rod."

I grasped her prick with two hands and engulfed her head in my mouth, sucking her pole feverishly while I slathered her shaft with my tongue. At the same time, Shae wrapped her arms around my ass and pulled me tightly toward her, encircling my bud in her mouth. We both moaned, thrashing our hips against each other's faces.

As we pressed our bodies together with our tits sliding against each other's abdomens, I rejoiced in the knowledge that I was making love to someone I'd never imagined being with in my wildest fantasies. It felt strange to be sucking a cock that didn't belong to a man for a change and to feel someone kissing me in my most intimate areas that wasn't a regular woman. It was like she had some kind of super-power, like she was my very own *Wonder Woman*.

As our moaning began to rise in urgency and volume, and our pleasure arced inexorably toward orgasm, I slipped my hand inside Shae's pussy and curled my fingers toward her G-spot. She hummed excitedly, thrusting her cock deeper into my mouth, and I tried to relax my throat to take as much of her as possible. Normally, I'd gag on a man's dick this size, but somehow with Shae I didn't have the same sense of fear being taken advantage of by someone far stronger than me. I knew that Shae would be gentle with me, not fucking my face just to get her rocks off. We were truly making love to one another, and I savored every moment feeling her warm, throbbing organ in my mouth.

I could feel myself nearing the point of no return as she teased my burning clit with her tongue, sucking and teasing my nub as she squeezed my buttocks with her hands.

"Mmm-mmm," I grunted, signaling that I was about to come.

"Mmm-*hmm*," Shae nodded, clenching her buttocks as I relaxed my throat while she sank her cock all the way into my mouth.

Suddenly, the walls of her pussy began contracting against my fingers as I felt her pole pulsing while she poured her jism down my throat. Feeling her coming both ways soon put me over the edge, and I groaned as I clamped down hard and sprayed my juices onto her face, coming in a series of powerful contractions that never seemed to stop. All the while, we gnashed our tits against each other's tummies, feeling every square inch of our bodies tingling in euphoria.

I held Shae in my arms until her contractions subsided then I drew my head back, closing my lips around her crown. I wanted to taste her for the first time—even her *milk* tasted sweet and creamy.

"Mmm," I purred, feeling her pussy twitching as I milked the last drops out of her trembling hard-on.

Shae kept her face planted between my legs while she caressed my ass and nibbled on my jewel. As we held each other lovingly in our arms, there was no longer any doubt in either of our minds that we'd created something special and neither one of us wanted to pull away anytime soon. Within a few minutes, we both drifted off to sleep, dreaming of nymphs and mermaids gliding through an ethereal realm.

5

———

When we woke up a few hours later, we snuggled next to each other, kissing softly and talking about our plans for the future. We were both giddy as schoolgirls talking about all the places we wanted to go and all the different adventures we wanted to have. But before long, we realized how much of an appetite we'd worked up, and we went downstairs where I cooked up some fresh seafood and prepared the cucumber salad. When we finished, Shae looked at me and smiled.

"That was a lovely dinner, Jade," she said, raising a playful eyebrow. "But now we don't have one of your favorite sex toys to play with any longer. Whatever are we going to do with ourselves?"

"Oh, I've got plenty of *other* toys to play with," I said, looking at her with a mischievous grin. "Why don't we go back upstairs and see what we can find to work with? I'm intrigued to see how we can incorporate some of them with your special features."

"I'm guessing you don't have too many cock rings or

Fleshlights in your bedroom," she grinned. "They're probably all designed for clitoral or vaginal stimulation."

"I think we might be able to find a way to make a few of them work for both of us," I said, grabbing her hand. "Come on, I've got a few ideas I want to try out."

When we got back upstairs, I pulled open my nightstand and showed Shae my collection of sex toys and dildos. Most of them looked like the normal female stimulators you'd find at any sex shop, but there was one that she seemed particularly interested in.

"What's this thing?" she said, picking up a long silicone wand with a bulb on the end and a mysterious hole in its base.

"That's one of my favorite sex toys," I smiled. "It's called an Osé vibrator, and it works in a very unique way."

"How so?" Shae said, placing the tip of her finger into the little hole.

"Let me *show* you instead," I said, pulling it away from her. "I've got a special idea for how we can adapt it for you to use." I shimmied up against the bed's headboard and spread my legs, tapping the mattress between my thighs. "Sit in front of me and rest your back against my chest. I think you might kind of like this."

Shae peered into my eyes and smiled.

"I'd like *anything* we do together," she said. "As long as I'm lying next to you."

"This time, it will be a little different. It'll give me a chance to stimulate and explore *every* part of you at the same time."

"Mmm, I like the sound of that," Shae said, shifting her ass up next to my crotch.

I could see her cock angled at half-mast, unsure of what to expect. I grasped the Osé vibrator and slowly bent the flexible wand in the reverse direction. Unlike its normal use in the missionary position with the wand curled upward to stimulate a woman's G-spot while the other part caressed her clit a few inches higher, in *Shae's* case we'd have to make some adjustments. For one thing, she didn't have a clit to stimulate, but she was also faced in the opposite direction, so the wand would have to be turned the other way around.

I reached down and caressed the sides of her lips to prepare her for the insertion. She'd have to be good and wet to enjoy the tool's unique movement, but I also wanted to get her fully hard so I could play her *other* part while she was being stimulated internally.

"Mmm," she purred. "I like it when you stroke me like that. It makes me feel very...womanly."

"Oh you're a *woman*, alright," I said, slipping my fingers inside her box to see how wet she was becoming. "A *super* woman–my own very special action hero."

"Mmm," she panted, rocking her hips against my fingers deep inside her. "You know I'd protect you against anyone who'd try to take you away from me."

"You don't have to worry about any of that, sweetheart. I'm stuck on you like glue now, remember?"

"Right, hormones, and all that," she smiled, turning her head toward me. "But right now, I'm stuck on you in a very different way."

"You *like* that?" I said. "Do you like the feeling of my fingers fucking your pretty pussy?"

"Yes, Jade," she sighed, resting her head against my chest. "Fuck me with your fingers while I play with my cock."

As she moved her hand up toward her throbbing pole now flapping straight up against her tummy, I batted it away gently.

"Let *me* have the pleasure," I said. "I'm going to have my hands freed up soon enough."

"Oh?" Shae teased, looking at the strange sex toy lying on the bed a few inches from her watering pussy.

"I think you're about ready to try this thing," I said, picking it up and pointing the bulbous tip toward her opening.

I turned it around with the hole facing her anus, then inserted the tip slowly into her slit. Shae tilted her hips forward to accept the instrument and hunched down a few inches to allow it to penetrate all the way inside her.

"Mmm," she purred. "That's a pretty big cock you're wielding there, my love. But I'm not sure it can do all the things your fingers can do for me."

"I wouldn't be too sure about that," I grinned, reaching down to tap the button on the base of the unit with my finger. The device began humming, and Shae's body jerked in surprise as she twisted her head to look at me with wide eyes.

"What the *hell*?" she said. "What is that thing? It doesn't feel like any vibrator I've used before."

"It's not really a vibrator," I said. "As you're about to see. It's more of a human *simulator*. Can you feel it caressing the inside of your pussy?"

"Yes," Shae said. "It feels like a finger stroking me. A very long and *soft* finger."

"I knew I'd be able to make you forget about my own fingers soon enough," I smiled. "I've got other plans for them."

Part of the attraction of using the special vibrator with Shae was that it would free up my hands to play with her cock while her pussy was being stimulated in other ways. I wanted to feel her burning flesh in my hands again while I watched her hips trembling from the feeling she was receiving inside. In her position faced away from me, it gave me an opportunity to caress every part of her body while the sex toy did its work on her lower parts.

I poured some baby oil into my palms and encircled her python with both hands as I began pumping her shaft up and down while the Osé finger caressed the inside wall of her pussy. Shae threw her head back against my chest in pleasure and I plunged my tongue into her mouth, kissing her passionately while she was being serviced below. I could feel her hips cavitating wildly against my crotch as she received stimulation simultaneously in both of her erogenous zones. As she rocked her body against my hands and the finger probing deep inside her pussy, I watched her pretty tits bouncing on her chest.

"*Fuck*, Jade," she hissed. "That feels incredible. I've never–"

"Been fucked and caressed at the same time?"

"Not like this," she panted.

"Mmm," I said, taking one hand off her cock and squeezing her breast while I twisted my other hand around the tip of her pole. "I like being able to feel and touch all of your parts this way."

"Fuck yes," she squealed, pumping her big dick into my hand. I could see precum pouring out the top of her slit, and the mix of her creamy emission with the watery baby oil made for an even silkier lube. "I can't imagine anything more heavenly than having you caressing every sensitive part of my body."

I grinned at her devilishly as I reached between her legs to tap the button on the base of the Osé vibrator one more time.

"I'm not quite sure we've finished caressing *every* sensitive part of your body," I said.

Suddenly, a snake-like appendage hidden under the hole of the vibrator emerged and began licking her twitching anus with its realistic tongue-like action.

"*Uhhn!*" Shae groaned, flexing her abs as she pressed her hips harder against the device. "What the hell is *that*?"

"I told you this was a special vibrator that was capable of stimulating you in many places. Just sit back and enjoy while you let *both* of us pleasure every part of your sexy body."

Shae leaned back against my chest and rested her head against my shoulder as I watched her face grow redder and redder from the rising tide of pleasure within her. I glanced down at her throbbing member and saw some pulses of precum dribbling over the top of her crown and down the underside of her shaft. I placed my other hand back on her throbbing meat and began pumping it tightly between my two fists. As I watched her purple head poking in and out of my hands, a bright flush began to spread over the top of her chest.

Suddenly, her face tightened up and her stomach muscles flexed as her body jerked against mine. While I pumped her raging dick and the Osé wand caressed her G-spot, with its tongue teasing her quivering rosebud, she wailed at the top of her lungs and wrapped her hands around mine as her prick jetted thick streams of white cum high into the air. I watched with amazement as she ejected one long string after another, arcing high into the air before landing with a loud plop onto her shaking chest.

When she finally stopped cumming, I took my hands off her cock and rubbed the creamy dew all over her plump tits and hard nipples. I'd never seen anything so erotic in all my life, and to have held her in my arms while I beheld the spectacular fireworks show was just icing on the cake. I turned my head to kiss her gently, and she squeezed her hands three times against mine still wrapped around her throbbing member as if to say 'I love you.'

I squeezed her pole three times back to return the sentiment as I watched the last bit of cum dribble over the tip of her magnificent flute.

That's one instrument I'm never going to get tired of playing, I said to myself as I held her softly in my arms.

Everybody's an exhibitionist in disguise...

Spying on the neighbors just got a lot more interesting...

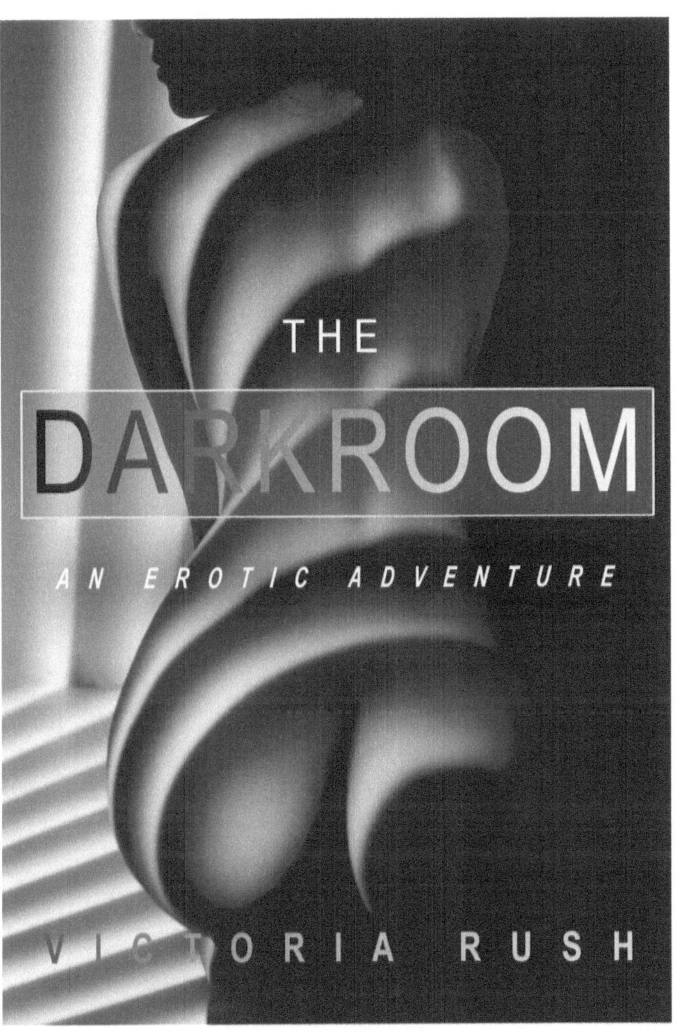

Everything's sexier in the dark...

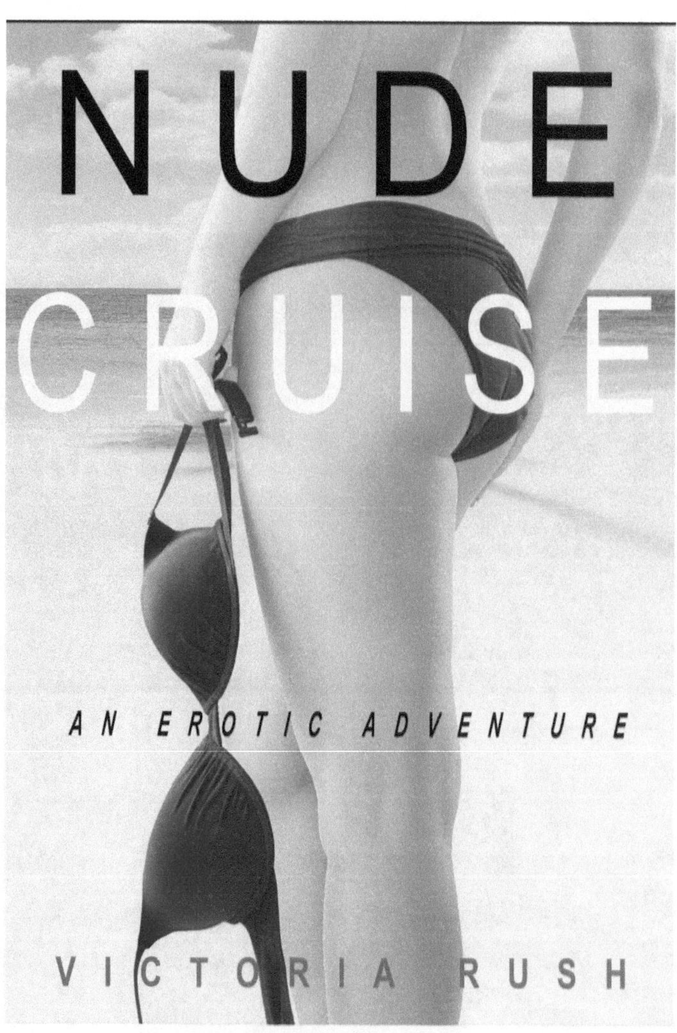

Some people get wet on a cruise for different reasons...

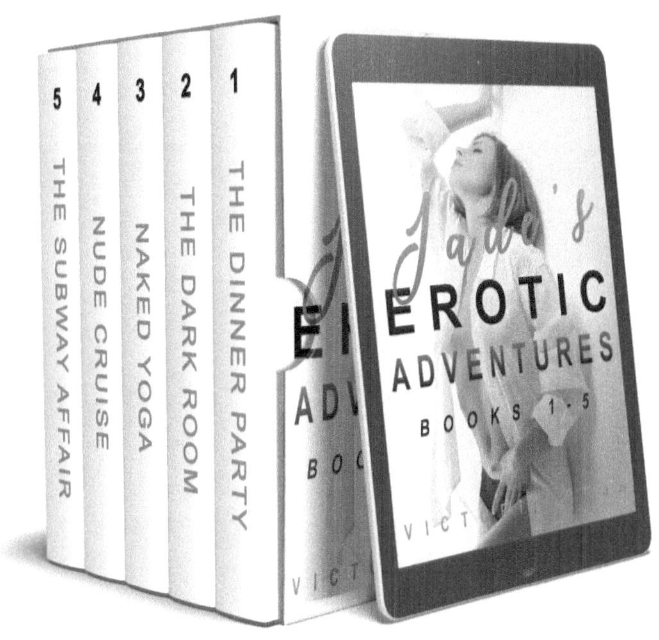

Books 1 -5 in the bestselling series - 60% off

THE DINNER PARTY - PREVIEW
FINGER FOOD

Sometime later, I heard a soft tap on my bedroom door. Not wanting to remove myself just yet from my cocoon of luxury, I called out to answer.

"Yes?"

"It's time for your massage," a woman's voice replied.

"Just one minute please."

I reluctantly stepped out of the bath and quickly toweled myself dry. I wrapped a large bath sheet around me, re-donned my mask, then opened the bedroom door.

A petite young Asian girl greeted me, wearing a kimono similar to mine and a crimson masquerade mask.

Apparently not everybody who works here always walks around stark naked.

The girl was utterly breathtaking. Long jet-black hair cascaded over high cheekbones past pouty lips, her delicate collarbones peeking from the top of her kimono. I could see her breasts and hips outlined by the tightly-wrapped kimono and suddenly wished that she too had come to my boudoir naked.

"My name is Jasmine," she said. "I'm your personal

masseuse and esthetician. Are you ready for your final preparation?

Just the thought of this beauty laying her tender hands on me sent a shiver down my spine.

"Definitely. Please come in. How would you like me to prepare?"

"Come with me, please."

Jasmine led me into the bathroom, where she nonchalantly removed her kimono and hung it behind the bathroom door.

Oh my God.

I didn't think anyone in this place could get more beautiful or sensuous. Jasmine had perfectly shaped B-cup breasts with a thin indentation running down the center of her perfectly toned stomach. Like everyone else in this place, her pubis was utterly bald and flawless. She barely looked eighteen and I was just about to ask her age, but she spoke first.

"If you'd like to remove your towel and lay face down on the table, we can get started. May I call you Jade?"

There was something about her confident manner and tone that belied her youthful appearance. I had no inhibitions whatsoever about displaying myself unclothed to this stranger.

"Yes, thank you, Jasmine." I unhooked my bath sheet and threw it against the side of the tub.

"Would you like me to drape your backside?" Jasmine asked.

"That won't be necessary," I quickly answered.

Jasmine walked over to the vanity counter and picked up two small bottles of oil resting under an orange radiant lamp. She brought them back to the massage table, opened one, and poured the oil into one cupped hand then rubbed her hands together. The scent of lavender wafted toward my nose.

I closed my eyes in anticipation of her touch. I'd had massages before, but nothing as sensuous and stimulating as this. When her hands touched the small of my back, I jerked reflexively from the sexual tension. My heart was beating a hundred miles an hour as I felt the blood coursing through my veins.

Jasmine must have sensed my nervous tension and began pressing her fingers more firmly into my back as she moved them slowly up each side of my spine. The warm oil allowed her hands to glide effortlessly across my skin. She used every surface of her hands to massage my muscles, expertly kneading my skin with her fingers and palm.

I began to relax as my muscles softened and surrendered to her touch. She sensuously massaged every part of my back, shoulders, and neck, applying just the right amount of pressure. Periodically, she would pour more warm oil on my lower back, dipping her hands in it to replenish the silky lubrication against my pliant skin.

Just as the sexual tension began to subside from the utter relaxation of the massage, Jasmine moved her hands down to my buttocks and began to caress them in soft circular motions. My glutes contracted involuntarily and I unconsciously pressed my mound into the firm padding of the table. Suddenly I was quickly reminded that a gorgeous young woman was caressing my naked body. She cupped each buttock between her hands as she massaged my ass tantalizingly, her little finger sliding slowly into the cleft just above my anus.

Periodically, I'd partially open one of my eyes with my head turned in her direction to look at her gorgeous body. My head was at the same level as her midsection, and my mouth watered as I watched her stomach muscles flex and her hips undulate with each movement of her hands. At times her pussy was almost right beside me and I wanted to reach out and run my own fingers up her soft legs.

I was in total heaven and getting wetter by the moment. Just when I thought I couldn't stand it anymore, she suddenly moved her hands down to my feet and began massaging her thumbs into my soles.

I'd always loved having my feet massaged, but nobody did it like Jasmine. She cradled my foot and used every part of her hands to massage and knead every surface from my heel to my toes. I didn't want her to stop, but there were other parts of my body that were screaming for attention.

As if reading my thoughts, she began moving her hands up toward my calf, using her thumbs to spread the muscle apart. She lingered almost as long on my calf as she had on my foot, rolling the ball of my calf between both of her hands, sliding her slick hands up and down erotically. I couldn't help imagining how she might use those same hands to massage a man's erect cock in a similar manner. My mind wandered again to what pleasures lay in wait for me over dinner.

After shifting her hands to my right leg and giving my other foot and calf similar attention, she placed each hand just behind my knees and began to slowly move them up towards my buttocks. Her thumbs pressed against my inner thighs as she glided tantalizingly close to my apex.

I rolled my legs outward in an invitation to move closer. My legs were parted enough that I was sure she could see my vulva from her vantage point behind me. In my highly aroused state, my lips were engorged and spread apart, revealing my moist and quivering opening.

But as much as I desperately wanted her to, Jasmine

never touched me there. She repeatedly slid her hands right up to the edge of my slit, pressing and rotating her thumbs on the fleshy meat of my upper thighs just below my aching pussy. I suppose this was part of her master plan—to tease me mercilessly and inflame my passions so I'd be ready for just about anything at the main event.

It was certainly working. After thirty minutes of Jasmine's ministrations, I was grinding my pussy into the table trying desperately to give my clit some needed direct stimulation.

Just when I thought I couldn't be teased any more tantalizingly, Jasmine opened one of the bottles of warm oil and poured it directly into the crack of my ass. She paused as the fluid flowed down and directly over my parted lips. I almost came from the gentle movement of the warm liquid as it trickled across the folds of my labia, channeled toward the junction where they joined together at my clit. I shuddered in pleasure at the feeling, even if it was only the subtlest of touch.

Jasmine suddenly interrupted my thoughts.

"Would you like to turn over now?"

It was the first time she had spoken directly to me since the massage started, and it surprised me in my catatonic, pre-orgasmic state. I practically flipped over like a fish out of water and spread my legs expectantly. Finally, I'd get some relief. Surely, she couldn't leave me hanging like this.

"It's time for your final grooming," she said. "I'll need you to part your legs a bit further to provide full access."

Grooming? I knew this was part of the process, but somehow it didn't seem fair to transition at this precise moment. At least I'd be able to stay on the comfortable massage table instead of the clinical vinyl chairs used by my regular esthetician.

Jasmine walked over to another cabinet by the makeup table and withdrew a leather bag from one of the drawers, then brought it back to the table. She reached into the bag and pulled out a cordless hair trimmer.

"Do you have a preference regarding your appearance?" she asked. "Do you prefer natural, neatly trimmed, or bare?"

I knew she was referring to my pubic hair, which I generally kept neatly trimmed. I'd always thought going fully bald was unnatural and unseemly, catering to men's prurient fantasies of fucking young schoolgirls. But in this situation, it seemed entirely appropriate, like I was stripping away all my camouflage and armor.

If tonight was all about being watched, I might as well bare myself in every sense of the word and truly let my inhibitions go. I began to fantasize about rubbing my bare pussy against Jasmine's while she poured warm oil between us. The more work she had to do on me, the more chance I'd have to make this last and hopefully get off.

I didn't hesitate. "Bare, thank you."

"As you wish," she said. "I'll remove the long hairs first with the trimmer, then shave you smooth with a razor."

No waxing? This was different. I was relieved to not have to bear the painful and violent trial of having my hairs ripped out en masse. Although shaving down there was always a scary proposition, I felt safe in the capable and practiced hands of this beautiful esthetician.

Jasmine nodded, then flipped a switch on the trimmer. The device buzzed softly as she placed it gently on my mound. I had only a light dusting of fur and it didn't take long for her to remove it with a few short strokes over my pubis. I shuddered as the vibrations penetrated deep into my core. If she had placed the flat head on my clitoris, I would have popped off in a millisecond. Instead, she turned the trimmer face-down and gently swiped the vibrating teeth against the sides of my vulva, sensuously separating my labia with her hands as she moved the device between my legs to trim the hairs on the inside and outside of my labia.

It was an insanely titillating feeling, but just clinical enough to bring me down from my plateau and shift my focus. My mind wandered to the upcoming feast, and I contemplated what surprises lay in wait at the main event. The hostesses had suggested there would be 'contact' of some sort during the meal, and I was intrigued exactly who and how it would be administered. The idea of being fully bald, cleansed, and thoroughly stimulated going into the event was an incredible rush.

Jasmine continued with the trimmer all the way down my perineum to my anus, barely touching me with the trimmer so as not to pinch any delicate tissues. Apparently there were no parts of my erogenous zone that would remain untouched, now—and perhaps later.

She turned off the trimmer and placed it at the foot of the table. Then she took a bottle of gel from the bag and spread the gel on her hands. Using both hands, she spread it gently between my legs, starting on my mound all the way down to my rosebud.

My body almost levitated above the table as Jasmine finally laid her hands directly on my clitoris. The gel had a mild stinging quality that added to the stimulating sensation. If this was meant to excite my follicles in preparation for the shave, it wasn't the only feature of my anatomy that it made erect. I could feel the hood of my clitoris retract as my button filled with blood and began to push outward. Suddenly, I was fully stimulated again and lusting for Jasmine's touch. I fantasized about her bending down and taking my swollen nub between her puffy lips and letting me come in her mouth.

Unfortunately, my satisfaction would have to wait a little longer. Instead, Jasmine reached into her bag and pulled out a straight-edge razor. In anyone else's hands, it might look threatening, especially in my prostrated and vulnerable position. But something about the way she delicately and sensuously opened the jackknifed tool instantly evaporated my fears. I could see how this type of razor would in fact give her better control safely cutting my stubs instead of the usual ladies plastic razor.

With her right hand, Jasmine gently laid the razor on its flat edge at the top of my mound, while she gently pulled my skin upwards with her other hand. Then she slowly turned the sharp edge perpendicular to my skin and began softly scraping the razor downwards. I could hear the bristling sound as the razor edge removed my nubs right down to the follicles. She repeated the pattern in one inch wide swipes on one side then the other of my pubis, being ever-so-careful to stop just where my clitoris lay quivering in a mixture of fear and excitement. There was something about the utter vulnerability of the procedure that made it the most erotic experience I'd ever had.

Jasmine used the same deft touch as she moved down my vulva and perineum, scraping the vestiges of stray hairs away with gentle swipes of the long blade, while sensuously separating my folds and flesh with her other hand. She took extra time and care around my anus and clit, using the gentlest and slowest motion I've ever felt someone apply to my body. The combination of fright and titillation as she probed my most sensitive body parts created a river of sensuous fluids running down my vulva. By this time, no shaving gel was necessary to provide a smooth gliding surface for the knife.

When she was finished, Jasmine retrieved a fresh wash towel from beside the sink and held it under the warm water faucet then twisted the excess water into the basin. She returned to the table and placed it over my splayed legs then gently cleansed the excess moisture and remaining shaving gel with gentle massaging movements of her hands. The warm, moist towel felt exquisite against my newly shaved skin. Jasmine's hands now felt comforting between my legs rather than erotic.

She had taken me on an incredibly sensuous erotic arc, right to the edge of ecstasy and back, to a quiet relaxed place. I exhaled fully and completely for the first time in almost an hour.

Jasmine removed the towel from between my legs and held up a large hand mirror at a forty-five degree angle toward me.

"What do you think?" she asked.

I tilted my head up and studied her masterpiece. Far from the usual red and swollen vulva that I typically experienced after the violent waxing with my regular esthetician, I'd never seen my pussy look so beautiful. Utterly bereft of any hair, my entire perineum from my pubic mound to my anus was totally bald, pink—and gorgeous. I just stared at my beautiful pussy, utterly transfixed by the transformation.

"You have to *feel* it to really appreciate how beautiful you are, Jade," Jasmine purred.

I moved my right hand down, running my fingers along the edges of my pussy. I gasped from a feeling I'd never felt before. It felt smooth as silk: no bumps or blemishes or cuts or bruises. It was almost as if I was feeling somebody else— somebody I'd never felt before. I couldn't stop my left hand joining the other in rubbing and caressing my sensitive organs.

Jasmine lowered the mirror and smiled at me as I felt the moisture begin to accumulate between my legs again.

"It's almost time for your dinner appointment," she said. "Why don't you save the best for last? I think you'll find plenty of ways to satisfy your appetite over the next couple of hours."

She lifted my kimono from the hook at the edge of the bathtub and held it open for me.

"I'll escort you downstairs now if you're ready. All you need to bring is your kimono and slippers—and your mask of course."

I sat up slowly and stepped off the massage table. Turning around, I held my arms out as Jasmine lifted one arm of the silk robe onto me then the other. Then she turned around to face me, wrapped the silk tie around me, and tied a single bow over my belly button. She retrieved my matching silk slippers and knelt down on one knee to gently lift my feet one at a time and place them softly inside. It took every ounce of my power not to grab her head and pull it into my pulsating pussy.

Jasmine stood up gracefully and smiled into my eyes.

"If you'll follow me, I'll escort you now to the fantasy feast."

She didn't bother putting her own robe on. Her tight little ass barely jiggled as she stepped smartly ahead of me. I wasn't sure if I'd have a chance to feel Jasmine's touch again before the evening was over, but for now I was in total bliss ogling her petite, curvaceous figure from behind...

Read More

ABOUT THE AUTHOR

If you would like to receive notification of new book(s) in Jade's Erotic Adventures, follow me at http://bookbub.com/authors/victoria-rush.

If you have a moment, please post a brief review on my Amazon book page at viewbook.at/ladyboy . Even just a couple of sentences will help other readers find and enjoy this book as much as you hopefully did.

Follow, share, like, and comment at:

www.facebook.com/authorvictoriarush
www.pinterest.com/authorvictoriarush
www.twitter.com/authorvictoriarush
authorvictoriarush@outlook.com

Hope to see you again soon!

www.ingramcontent.com/pod-product-compliance
Lightning Source LLC
Chambersburg PA
CBHW030822200726
48288CB00004B/1353